S0-BUA-216

Written by Shannen Yauger

Illustrated by Anita Schmidtt

Cover design by Phillip Colhouer

© 2020 Jenny Phillips

goodandbeautiful.com

Chapter One

Once upon a time, in a
faraway land near the Great
Green Forest, sat a little
log cabin. This little log
cabin had a bright red roof,
purple pansies planted

near the door, and a little path made of river rocks that led from the cabin to the Great Green Forest.

Inside this little log cabin, laughter could often be heard, for in it lived a girl named Gwenndolyn. "Gwennie the Adventurer," as she was so often called by Mother and Father,

always had a smile on
her face and a song in her
heart. Her brown braids
bounced when she walked,

and her little green eyes always sparkled.

Gwennie had seven small sisters who all loved to run and play along the path and in the forest. They went on adventures in the trees

and made friends with the animals of the Great Green Forest. Squeaky Squirrel, Chipper Chipmunk, and Darting Deer all loved Gwennie and her seven small sisters.

As often as she could, Gwennie would pack a picnic to take into the forest. She would bring nuts for Squeaky Squirrel and Chipper Chipmunk, apples for Darting Deer, and Mother would make little cheese sandwiches for her and her seven small sisters. It made her happy to feed her furry friends well, before the cold of the snowy winter arrived, and to see her sisters laugh and play amongst the animals.

One sunny Saturday, after finishing her daily chores, Gwennie asked Mother if she could take her seven small sisters into the Great Green Forest.

"Yes," said Mother, "but be back before dark!"

Smiling softly, Gwennie packed her big blue basket, slipped into her sweater, and dressed her seven small sisters for an adventure.

❧ Chapter ❧ Two

"What shall we discover today?" Gwennie sang sweetly as she carried her big blue basket out the door of the little log cabin, with her seven small sisters

merrily trailing behind.
They followed the river
rock path to the Great
Green Forest. The forest
smelled rich today, as the
leaves were just starting
to turn autumn colors and
fall, making a red and gold
blanket on the ground.

"Crunch! Crunch!
Crunch!" could be heard

under the girls' feet as they started their adventure.

They skipped and they sang. They sang and they skipped. Gwennie swung her big blue basket as she twisted and twirled through the Great Green Forest.

Suddenly, she stopped. In all of her singing and skipping, twisting and twirling, she had lost the trail and was now deep in the Great Green Forest.

Her seven small sisters
still twisted and twirled,
skipped and sang, and did
not know that Gwennie was
scared.

"Wait, please," called
Gwennie. Her seven small
sisters stopped twisting
and twirling. They were
surprised to hear the fear
in Gwennie's voice.

"Oh! Where is the trail?" Gwennie spoke again, a little softer this time. There was no answer, other than the sound of the leaves blowing in the breeze and the sniffles of her seven small sisters.

"Don't be scared," said Gwennie, as she saw their tears. She sat down with her seven small sisters.

They all piled in for a hug.

"I can find our way home."

She looked around at the ground, hoping to see her footprints on the forest floor. Carefully, she tried to retrace her twists and twirls in her mind, but she was unable to do so. Gwennie was lost with her seven small sisters deep in the Great Green Forest. She dropped her head, as her normally merry eyes filled with fear.

Chapter Three

"Squeak!" she heard.
Gwennie raised her head.
There, on the lowest limb of
a tall pine tree, sat Squeaky
Squirrel. He turned his
head from side to side,

squeaking at Gwennie's basket. Her seven small sisters squealed in delight.

"Look, Gwennie! He knows we brought his food, and he must be hungry!" they said.

"It's not time for a picnic, Squeaky Squirrel," said Gwennie with concern, as she stood up. "We are lost in the Great Green Forest, and I told Mother we would be home before dark!" She walked over to a mossy rock to sit, then felt a tickle on her ankle. Chipper Chipmunk was frolicking by her feet. He pounced onto her picnic basket and looked at her.

"Oh, Chipper Chipmunk, there won't be a picnic today," said Gwennie, as she grew more upset. "We are lost in the Great Green

Forest, and I told Mother we would be home before dark!" She covered her face with her hands as her seven small sisters sat down by her feet.

"Is this still an adventure, Gwennie?" asked the smallest sister. Gwennie stopped covering her face and smiled at her softly.

She remembered that she is known as Gwennie the Adventurer, and that she must be brave.

"Yes, and what an adventure this is!" she

replied, so that the smallest sister would not be scared. She hugged her smallest sister to her, looked around, and the merry sparkle returned to her eyes.

After a moment, Gwennie heard the snap of a twig and the crackle of the leaves on the ground. She looked to her left to see soft brown eyes peek through the bushes. "Oh, Darting Deer, are you looking for your food as well?" Gwennie's stomach growled. She remembered that her furry friends needed to eat before the chill of winter arrived.

"I guess we should all eat, shouldn't we? We need not go hungry while we are lost in the Great Green Forest." Gwennie opened her big blue basket. Her seven small sisters gathered around her.

"Oh!" Gwennie exclaimed, peering into the picnic basket. "Where are the nuts?

Where is the apple? What has happened to our bread and cheese that Mother wrapped for our meal?" She looked around. She could not find any of the food she had so carefully put together.

*Chapter *Four

Her seven small sisters did not understand. "We are hungry!" they said. "We have twisted and twirled, skipped and sung, and now our poor tummies are grumbly!" Gwennie did not know what to say, so she gave them each a hug instead. "I will find some food, small sisters. Let me be still a moment to think." She sat on the mossy rock once more.

Her seven small sisters sat around her, quietly waiting. Chipper Chipmunk, after peeking into the picnic basket, scampered a few feet away and stopped.

He stared at Gwennie and tilted his furry head to the side.

He ran to her, then ran back to where he had stopped before. Gwennie's

seven small sisters stood up to try to see where he went, though they did not leave Gwennie's side.

Squeaky Squirrel also peered into the picnic basket, then ran to stand beside Chipper Chipmunk. He stopped and stared at Gwennie, too.

"Oh, my furry friends, are

you upset that I do not have your food? Are you hungry as well?" Gwennie's tummy gave another loud growl as she looked around.

The day was passing by, and it was not quite as bright in the Great Green Forest.

Darting Deer slowly came up to Gwennie. He looked

at her with his beautiful brown eyes, then twitched his tail and walked over to Squeaky Squirrel and Chipper Chipmunk. All three animals quietly watched Gwennie and her seven small sisters.

Chapter Five

As the sounds of the Great
Green Forest grew quieter
and the sun dropped lower
in the sky, Gwennie quietly
watched the animals. They
seemed to be waiting. She

looked at her sisters. The smallest of the seven small sisters moved first. She went to where the animals stood. Chipper Chipmunk pounced around by her

foot. She looked down at the ground.

"Gwennie, look!" said the smallest sister. "It is a nut!" Slowly, Gwennie stood up. She wiped away a tear, picked up her big blue basket, and walked to where the animals and her smallest sister stood.

"Oh!" Gwennie exclaimed.

She picked up the nut. Her stomach grumbled and growled. She looked at the nut and down at the little chipmunk. She thought of her warm home and the smell of fresh bread. She thought of the cold winter and how hard it must be for Chipper Chipmunk to find food. She smiled at

the smallest sister, who
nodded her head as if
she understood, and then
carefully handed the fat
nut to Chipper Chipmunk.
He stuffed it into his cheek
and scampered ahead, just
around the twisted tree.
Again, he stopped. And
again, the other animals
followed him. Gwennie

and all of her seven small sisters followed the animals.

"Here is another nut from my basket!" Gwennie cried, pointing at the ground.

She picked up the nut and looked carefully at it, then handed this one to Squeaky Squirrel. She stepped forward.

"And another!" she

exclaimed. "And, look, here is the apple!"

The seven small sisters all clapped and cheered. They could feed their animal friends!

Chapter Six

As the Great Green Forest grew darker, Gwennie walked forward while her furry friends scampered around the woods nearby. Her seven small sisters twisted and twirled along behind them, enjoying the great adventure again. All along the trail, she discovered bits and pieces of her picnic. With each little piece of food found, Gwennie and her seven sisters fed their furry friends.

Soon, she spotted the

bread and cheese, still wrapped in a little white napkin. Her seven small sisters stopped twisting and twirling. They all sat down by Gwennie as she handed out the cheese and bread. Gwennie knew that her seven small sisters were quite hungry, so she gave them all of her food

as well. They were quiet as they ate their dinner, just listening to the fading sounds of the Great Green Forest. It was now nearly dark, and the Great Green Forest was growing still.

"Gwennie, Mother said to be home by dark," said the smallest sister. She sounded scared.

"Yes, she did," Gwennie replied. "I made a mistake on my adventure, small sisters, and I am sorry. Now we need to be brave and find our way home." They finished their meal and stood up. Gwennie climbed onto a nearby stump to get a better view of the Great Green Forest in the last bit of daylight. She knew that an adventurer is always aware of what is around her. She peered through the trees.

Wait! Was that a light she saw off in the distance?

Chapter Seven

Gwennie gathered the big blue basket and her seven small sisters. Chipper Chipmunk, Squeaky Squirrel, and Darting Deer, their bellies now full, disappeared into the stillness of the Great Green Forest.

"Let's all hold hands as we skip along. No twisting and twirling, as it's harder to see at twilight," Gwennie explained. "We can sing, so that Mother can hear us and know that we are coming home."

Gwennie started singing:

"We set off on an adventure,

Twisting, twirling through the day.

But, alas, we lost the wooded path,

Our sunlight faded away!

We are on our way home,

Though the path we may not know.

But after we are rested,

On another adventure we will go!"

Her seven small sisters joined in, giggling.

Gwennie led the way, heading toward the light that was not so far off in the distance.

Just as the smallest sister said, "Gwennie, I am tired," the girls saw their cabin, with Mother standing in the lit doorway, awaiting their safe return.

"Girls!" Mother exclaimed. "Oh, I am so happy to see all of you!"

"I am sorry, Mother!" Gwennie exclaimed, as her small sisters danced around her. "We twisted and twirled, sang and skipped, and I am afraid I lost both our picnic and our way!"

"But, Mother," said the smallest sister, "it was a grand adventure! We found our food for our animal friends, ate our dinner in the dark, and sang our whole way home!"

The smallest sister smiled up at Gwennie. "We cannot wait for our next adventure!"

Mother wrapped Gwennie and her seven small sisters into a big bear hug. Once inside, Father and Mother ushered the seven small sisters upstairs for warm baths before bed. Gwennie ate a slice of bread and butter and had a mug of milk, as she was still quite hungry after feeding all of

the bread and cheese to her
seven small sisters.

With a sparkle in her eyes,
Gwennie stepped back
outside. It was dark now,
the only light coming from
the moon and stars and
the twinkling fireflies at
the edge of the Great Green
Forest. She left a big bowl
of nuts and two apples on a

tree stump, just in case the animals were still hungry too.

"I wonder," Gwennie thought to herself, "what tomorrow's adventure will bring!"

The End

MORE SILVER TALES FROM THE GOOD AND THE BEAUTIFUL LIBRARY

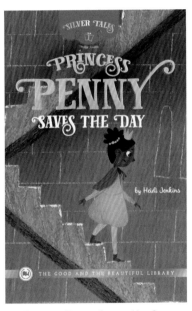

Princess Penny Saves the Day
By Heidi Jenkins

Peter the Persnickety
By Breckyn Wood